The edge of fear ...

The next evening was colder, and the clouds in the west looked red and angry. Cody gathered a bunch of boys from school in the town square and told them Ma's story. He then announced he was going to march up to Jackknife Hill with Pa's Bowie knife and stick it in Billy Herschel's grave, just as Jeb Pickering had done all those years ago. Only he wouldn't die like no coward at the hands of a dead man. He said we could come too, if we weren't too scared to watch, that was.

... cuts deep

The Edge

Of Midnight

Ghost Stories

by David R. Smith

Emma —
Keep the lights on!

— David R. Smith

This is a work of fiction. Names, characters, places and incidents are the products of the author's imagination or are used fictitiously, and any resemblance to actual persons, living or dead, business establishments, events or locales, is entirely coincidental.

Copyright © 2014 by David R. Smith
All rights reserved. No part of this book may be reproduced without permission from the author, David R. Smith, 15 East Ave., Livonia, NY 14487, excepting for brief passages appearing in a review for a newspaper or magazine.

ISBN: 978-1-312-64638-4

For ordering information, contact the author at drs32@rochester.rr.com or visit
www.lulu.com/davesbookstore

Printed in the United States of America

Book cover designed by Jennifer Hamson

For my dad,

who inspired me to pick up the pen

ACKNOWLEDGMENTS

Writers are influenced by other authors perhaps more than anybody else. To the late Ray Bradbury, for showing how fiction can be a vehicle for observing the terrain of human fear and hope. To the literary giants Madeleine L'Engle and C.S. Lewis for captivating me with the magic of science fiction and fantasy. And finally to Stephen King, who taught me that horror stories are more about us than the ghosts themselves.

A special debt of gratitude is owed to my mentor, Tim Wright, for steering me in the right direction. And to my wife, Jennifer, for supporting my literary endeavors. Finally, thank you to Julie Lawrence for a stellar job editing this book, and Jennifer Hamson for the superb cover art.

Contents

Introduction	8
The Ghost of the Hollow	14
Emily Brown	25
The Worst Kind of Mischief	35
The Secret of Langley Hall	43
The Thing in the Basement	58
Halloween Night	73
The Wind Breathes Cold	75
The Midnight Road	92

Introduction

What is the first thought to race through your mind when you hear a creak in the night? Is it just the timbers of the old house settling? Or are you imagining a restless ghost rummaging around in the attic?

If your thoughts turn immediately to the ghost, you are not alone. We are a nation of believers in spirits and haunts. At least one out of three Americans believe in ghosts. Despite all of our science and technology, many of us become as fearful of the dark as our cave-dwelling ancestors at the slightest hint of the paranormal. It takes no more than a footstep on a stair or a knock on a wall for our hearts to skip a beat and our adrenalin to spike. So why do we remain so stubbornly superstitious even now in the twenty-first century? Why are we drawn to ghost stories?

For centuries, tales of supernatural places and phenomena have been a part of American folklore. Most folks nowadays could tell a version of the ghostly hitchhiker story, where a man is terrified to find that the beautiful young woman he picks up late at night is actually dead. Or perhaps you've sat around a campfire and heard the story of the poor fool who takes a dare and visits the local cemetery at night, only to scare himself to death when he thinks he's seen a ghost!

And then there are accounts of historical hauntings, the ones based on actual events and often with eyewitnesses to back them up. For example, the phantom cannon fire and moaning specters of Gettysburg's battlefields. Or the poor souls of the falsely accused who met their end at the famously haunted Gallows' Hill in Salem, Massachusetts. Or any one of the hundreds of tales of haunted pubs, hotels, graveyards, and mansions all across the United States.

Ghost stories continue to enthrall us simply because they are, at heart, stories of human suffering, tragedy and redemption. They capture and magnify our passions, jealousies, foolishness and pride. A ghost story, in other words, is a window into the soul. And sometimes the view can be downright ugly. You could say that the greatest horror story is a life lived in service to one's own selfish desires.

In any case, no matter which century we live in, people are consistently human and rarely ever change. Fundamentally, we are a species given to both remarkable acts of compassion and despicable deeds of cruelty. And at the end of the day, ghost stories remind us that our actions have consequences. We can own them or ignore them, but we can never escape them.

In this anthology, I attempt to portray these themes as well as capture what I consider to be the essential elements of the best ghostly tales—a spooky atmosphere; lively storytelling; a dark undercurrent of foreboding. These are my innovations on classic American ghost lore, along with a few originals of my own thrown in for good measure.

In tales such as *Emily Brown* and *The Midnight Road*, you will meet ill-fated heroines who bear painful secrets. In *The Ghost of the Hollow*, the dark side of a young man's humor may be scarier than what his elders believe haunts the woods at night. And in *The Worst Kind of Mischief*, foolish choices on the part of a boastful teen leads to a regrettable, though not entirely undeserving, demise.

But I think I have taken enough of your time already. It is time to dim the lights, stoke the fire, and draw the curtains. Forget the wind rustling in the trees outside; it cannot harm you. Besides, if it isn't the wind, what can be done about it anyway?

Ghosts will conduct their business as they see fit. It is wise to simply stay out of their way.

However, if you should see a ghost, pay your humblest respects as you carry on your way.

And pray it goes haunting someplace else.

Words have no power to impress the mind without the exquisite horror of their reality.

-Edgar Allan Poe

O God! What a thing it is to be a ghost, cowering and shivering in an altered world, a prey to apprehension and despair!

-Ambrose Bierce

The Ghost of the Hollow

He was told not to enter the woods at night. All the children of the hollow were taught at a very young age to be afraid of the dark. But not everyone listened. Some were too foolish to heed the warnings of their elders.

Jacob Solomon was such a boy. For Jacob, life in the hollow was gloomy and depressing. A perpetual October land, where the days were endless and gray.

The winters were torturous and the summers too short to thaw the chill in his heart. Jacob dreamed of the day when he'd be eighteen, still some four years away. The day when he could pack whatever belongings could fit in his knapsack and ride out of town forever, maybe to someplace warm like Arizona or New Mexico. Or maybe he'd sail clear to the other side of the world. But in his heart of hearts he secretly feared that the superstition of the village elders was already entwined in his soul, and would follow him wherever he went.

With these sullen thoughts kicking around in his head, Jacob hurried down the dirt path from Silas Reed's place. The Solomon's closest neighbor, Silas occasionally employed Jacob to fix fence posts and shoe horses. Dusk was quickly scrubbing the daylight from the sky, and he knew he'd be in all kinds of trouble if he didn't make it back home before dark.

To save time, he took the shortcut through the woods. Like all residents of the hollow, he'd been raised to fear the noises of the woods, bred to believe the rustling sounds were a witch's cassock, the howls her animal familiars hunting for human prey.

Childish, stupid nonsense, Jacob thought, but he still looked over his shoulder at every fluttering wing and snapping twig behind him.

To his left he spotted the black iron gate surrounding the hollow's only graveyard. The legends warned that the spirits who resided there were restless and would chase away anyone who dared to enter the graveyard at night. It was said an old witch named Miranda came to the hollow long ago to escape persecution in the Salem witch trials, and lived out the rest of her lonely days in the woods near the cemetery. The legends spoke of her powers to change shape and cast spells, to even bring drought, famine and disease to the early settlers.

Jacob wasn't so sure. He was becoming a man, and a learned one at that, and he didn't think he believed in the unseen world of witches and ghosts anymore.

But there was only one way to find out, right? One thing he could do to prove his courage and his faith in the natural world.

He left the dirt path, trudged through the tall weeds, and stopped at the cemetery gate. There, he peered inside. The tombstones dripped with shadows, and the air was still and heavy. A wolf or mongrel of some sort bayed in the distance, too far away to be a threat. He became aware of his own quick breathing and told himself to remain calm. There were no ghosts with clanking chains around here, no witches riding broomsticks. The place was, well, *dead*, as you would expect it to be.

He laughed at his own private joke, and then the idea hit him. A way to pull an innocent little prank on his overbearing parents, who still insisted on treating him like a child fourteen years into his life.

With the sun now put to bed and the moon keeping watch over the night, Jacob dashed home, and not a moment too soon, for his parents were already waiting anxiously at the door.

"Where have you been?" boomed his father. He raised his eyebrows at Jacob's tousled hair and rumpled clothes. "What's happened to you, son?"

Jacob had been rehearsing his lines in his head the whole way home. "I was walking down the path by the cemetery," he panted. "I was hurrying so I wouldn't be late getting home, when I suddenly saw something through the trees." Here he paused for dramatic effect. "It was a ... a witch! She was wearing a black robe and had glowing silver eyes and knives in her hands. She was just floating there, watching me."

His mother and father exchanged startled glances.

Jacob continued: "Then she started moving toward me, cackling and scraping those knives together in her hands, like she wanted to chop me up and put me in her stew. I turned and ran but tripped, and that's when she fell upon me, grabbing my clothes and my hair and even tearing the sleeve of my coat." He showed them the seam of his jacket sleeve, the one he'd ripped intentionally just before emerging from the woods. Nothing made a story more convincing than a few props to go with it.

"My baby!" his mother bawled, as she swept him into her arms. Jacob buried his face in her shoulder to hide his smile.

"Thank God you're all right, son!" His father raised his lantern to the woods. "Let's get you inside and warm you by the fire."

Jacob followed his mother and father into the house. After a bowl of beef stew and a buttered roll, Jacob said he was going upstairs to retire for the night.

"Sleep well, Jake." His mother pecked him on the forehead when he lay down in bed, the way she had every night for fourteen years. "You're always safe here. Miranda can't get you while you're under *my* roof," she added fiercely.

Jacob closed his eyes and pretended to fall asleep. When he heard his mother retreat from the room and close the door behind her, he whisked the covers off and stared out his window. The moon had risen to the top of the sky, and in its chalky light Jacob imagined a whole army of witches, goblins and warlocks rampaging through the valley on a murderous spree. He grinned mischievously. It was time to put the next part of his prank into action.

In a voice loud and clear, he bellowed, "She's back! Help me, Miranda's outside my window! She's trying to get in!" Jacob dove under his sheets until his parents burst into the room. His father had a shotgun; his mother a frying pan.

"Where is she?" demanded his father. "I don't see—"

"There!" Jacob jumped out of bed and pointed to the window. "She was right out there, her face mere inches from the glass. I could see her pointy little black teeth, and her rotted skin. She had one gnarled hand up to the window, tapping. Oh father, can't you see her, standing there by the edge of the woods?"

His parents hurried over and looked, but then quickly shook their heads. Dismayed, his mother said, "Hyram, we need to do something about this before our boy is killed by that wicked thing!"

His father's jaw set in determination. "I know it. Get the lanterns, my other shotgun, some rope, and the dogs. We're goin' after her."

Jacob could barely control his glee.

Their hands full, Jacob and his parents followed the baying hound dogs into the woods. Even with the lanterns, the woods were so thick and dark it was like trying to see in a tunnel. His father said he knew a shortcut to the graveyard, and after what seemed like an eternity of picking carefully through scrub brush and weeds, they found themselves standing outside the cemetery gate, looking around and listening for any sign of the witch.

"I know you're out there!" His mother's fury was like a disturbed hornet's nest. "You cain't have my boy, y'hear me? He's mine! Now show us your ugly face so we can put a bullet in it!"

As Jacob's father cocked an ear to listen to the restless stirrings of the forest, his finger became jumpy on the trigger of the shotgun. Watching, Jacob wondered how much longer he should let the charade go on. Had he made his point yet? How much more could he take of his parents' foolishness and superstition? He was about to confess to the prank when a noise in the woods made them all jump. The dogs yipped, whined, and ran in circles, terrified. His father swung the shotgun around and pointed it at the darkness.

"Who's out there?" he bellowed. "Show yourself!"

A lumbering form appeared at the edge of the lamplight, moving toward them.

"Stop or I'll shoot!" The shotgun shook in his father's hands. "So help me I'll…"

BANG!

To Jacob's horror, the gun went off, and the figure in the woods slumped over and groaned. They rushed toward it, fearing the worst. As they brought the lamplight around, they saw old Silas Reed's ghastly face gawping up at them, pale with shock.

"I saw … the lights … heard … the dogs." He sputtered and coughed a mist of blood. "Came … to see if you … needed help. Why Hyram? *Why*?"

The old man's eyes emptied, and his body slowly took its final quivering breath.

His father stood resolutely. "Come," he said, tugging his wife away. "You shouldn't see this. I'll fetch the constable. It was an accident, but we're responsible." Jacob stayed crouched next to the body. He'd never seen death up close like this before. "Let's go, Jacob, and bring the dogs."

"But what about…?"

His father shook his head. "This witch hunt is over. At least for tonight."

His parents left, but Jacob couldn't move. This was his fault; *he* was to blame, not his father. He lost track of the time as he stared down at the body. Even the dogs gave up waiting, and searched out his mother and father on their own. Dogs knew better than to be alone in these particular woods at night.

From behind Jacob, in the depths of the forest, came the whooshing sound of wind stirring the trees. At first Jacob was barely aware of the rustling branches and chattering leaves, but when the chilled breeze caressed the back of his neck, he spun around to see what had touched him. There, he was confronted by the horrible sight of Miranda the witch, her silvery eyes boring into his own, reaching into the back of his mind and seizing his darkest fears. She slid past him, the air in her wake scented with the earthy dankness of the grave, and scooped poor Silas off the ground like a sack of feed. In her arms, he seemed to weigh as little as an acorn. She turned back to Jacob with a hideous smile.

"Thank you, Jacob Solomon," she rasped. Her teeth glinted like shiny razors in the black pit of her mouth. "I have not feasted in a long while."

And before he could say a word or turn to run, she was gone, the foul breeze trailing her back to whatever dreadful place she had come from.

After tonight, Jacob would never again doubt the presence of evil in the world.

Or, for that matter, in his own heart.

Emily Brown

In the town of Cooper's Mill there is a story about a girl named Emily Brown who died on the playground of St. Anne's Elementary School. Some say she was eight, others say ten or thirteen. Memories fade as the years drag on, but I don't suppose it matters much. Dead is dead. And Emily Brown has been lying underground for so long now—and her story told so many times around campfires by teenagers looking to scare themselves silly—that it has become a legend. That is, more fiction than fact.

We should let her poor soul rest in peace and move on, but folks 'round these parts can't seem to do that.

And that's because they say she lingers on, watching the school kids play. Sometimes you'll be on the swings and feel little hands give you a gentle push on your back. When you turn around, nobody's there. Other times, a strange footprint or handprint appears in the chalk dust next to yours, even when you're playing by yourself. And some kids say you can hear a little girl's earnest voice whisper "Be careful!" when you take your turn down the tall corkscrew slide. That's where they say Emily Brown had her accident, falling over the side and breaking her neck on the bed of wood chips below.

I can't say for certain that any of this is true. But I know a boy who claims he talked to Emily Brown.

His name is Brian Price, ten years old and in fifth grade at St. Anne's. He was playing by himself on the swings one afternoon when he saw a shadow out the corner of his eye. Believing it to be a bird or perhaps a strand of his own hair, he went back to humming a little song to himself when he realized his wasn't the only voice humming the tune. He looked to his left and there, on the swing beside his, appeared a girl in a navy blue St. Anne's jumper with straight black hair and sunken eyes. Brian's heart knocked with terror as the little girl smiled faintly at him. She kicked her feet up and swept forward. Soon she was swinging at the same speed as Brian, her haunted eyes gazing straight at his.

"Emily Brown?" he croaked. His mouth felt dry and his throat stiff. "Are-are you a ghost?"

She nodded slowly, and the smile drifted from her face. She now seemed much older and sadder to Brian, as though years had passed in mere seconds.

"What do you want?" Brian asked.

Emily Brown stopped swinging.

"Go to her," she told him, her voice as murky as her eyes. "Tell my mother her necklace is under the loose floorboard in my closet." Her desperate voice, so small yet so full of anguish, chilled Brian to the bone, but he knew instantly he had no choice. The look in Emily Brown's face shifted again. The cloud of melancholy lifted, and a desperate sense of urgency set in. She needed him to do this task, and he was not about to refuse her, no matter how scared or confused he felt.

"But where does your mother live?"

Emily opened her mouth as if she were going to answer, when all of a sudden she wavered like a heat mirage. Brian could see the grass and the trees and the sky straight through her body before she fragmented into wisps of smoke and disappeared. Stunned, he stayed where he was, staring at the swing and wondering what to do first. How would he find her address? Who *was* Emily Brown? All he knew were the local legends, and most of those were probably not even true.

Then it came to him. Sister Margaret Finley, of course! The principal of St. Anne's Elementary School knew just about everything about everyone in town. A high school English teacher for thirty years, she claimed that she taught the whole town how to conjugate verbs and interpret Shakespeare. First thing Monday morning Brian would go directly to her and get the answers he needed.

Brian barely slept that weekend, waiting for Monday morning to come. When it arrived, he hurried off the school bus and into Sister Margaret's office, where he found her staring oddly into space. She looked uncomfortable and exhausted.

"I had the strangest dream last night," she murmured to herself. Brian waited patiently in the doorway for her to explain, but when no explanation came, he cleared his throat and said, "Sister Margaret? Uh, can I ask you something?"

"I saw her again for the first time in … well, must be twenty years now," Sister Margaret continued in her odd, dreamy voice, as though she hadn't heard his question.

Brian shifted uncomfortably. He wasn't sure if he should stay or go. "Who did you see, Sister Margaret?" he finally asked. "Who are you talking about?"

"Poor Emily Brown," she answered, looking up and apparently noticing Brian for the first time. "She was watching me from the foot of the bed. There was a strange light in her eyes. She said, 'Help him. Tell him what he needs to know.' What do you suppose it all means, Brian?"

"I think I know." Brian crept into the office and sat down across from Sister Margaret, in the chair usually reserved for students who needed scolding. "I saw her two days ago on the playground," he explained. "I don't think she was trying to scare me. She told me to tell her mother—"

"—it's under the floorboard in the closet,'" Sister Margaret finished for him, her cheeks starting to pale. For the first time they made eye contact with each other. "We need to tell her, Brian. It might put Emily Brown's soul to rest once and for all."

Without another word, Sister Margaret led Brian outside to her car. They crossed town in a hurry to a quiet neighborhood where Brian had never been, and pulled up in front of a small rundown Cape Cod whose front lawn lay buried under a blizzard of scarlet maple leaves. A woman answered the door who could have been anywhere between sixty and one hundred. Her hollow eyes, gaunt skin and protruding cheekbones gave the impression of someone who hadn't eaten or slept well for a long time.

"Good morning, Anna," said Sister Margaret kindly. She gave Brian's hand a reassuring squeeze. "May we come in?"

The interior of the house was in the same condition as the outside—neglected and forlorn. They followed Anna to a gloomy parlor and sat down, billows of dust floating around their legs. "What do you both want?" asked Anna suspiciously.

"It's about Emily." Sister Margaret leaned forward. "We have a message from her."

Anna's eyes sharpened at once and slid over to Brian. "What do you mean, a *message*? My Emily died in a tragic accident over twenty years ago. Now her memory is a joke, a child's ghostly legend. What do you mean by coming here and taunting an old woman?"

As she was about to shoo them out, Brian shot to his feet. "Wait! In the closet, under a loose floorboard, there's a necklace. It's yours. I think Emily took it for some reason. She didn't say, but she wants you to have it back. Go and see."

Anna Brown's mouth flapped open and shut a few times in shock and exasperation at the boy's words. When at last she gave up on speech, she rose from her chair and left the living room. Sister Margaret and Brian followed. They went up the stairs and into a dimly lit bedroom in the back of the house, one with faded and cracked pink wall paper and dusty stuffed animals on the bed. Emily's old bedroom, Brian thought. Anna Brown went directly to the closet and flung open the doors. The small space was stuffed with toys, boxes, and clothes, which all three of them carefully pulled out. When the closet was cleared, Anna sank slowly and painfully on arthritic knees and started feeling along the cracks in the wooden boards. When one of them rattled loosely, she pried it up with her fingernails and reached into the dark space it exposed.

A moment later, she gasped in surprise! She pulled out of the floor a gold necklace with a heart-shaped pendant at the end. It gleamed in a beam of soft sunlight that suddenly thrust through a crack in the curtains, and made Brian's breath catch. Anna's eyes filled with tears. With trembling hands she undid the clasp and put the necklace on, grasping the pendant and murmuring a little prayer to herself. Sister Margaret knelt and prayed beside her, and when they were finished, Anna Brown looked up and smiled in gratitude at Brian.

"We'd had a fight the morning of her death," she explained, "and it all had to do with this necklace. My mother gave it to me when I was a child, so it was very valuable to me. One day Emily wanted to wear it to school. I told her no, but she protested, and stormed off with it against my wishes. After she died, I gave up hope of ever seeing it again. I have faith it will bring her soul peace knowing that I have it again. And, Brian, if you ever see her again, tell her I forgive her for hiding it from me, as I will tell her a thousand times in my prayers."

Brian promised he would, but it was a promise he didn't have a chance to keep, for Emily Brown's spirit was never seen again at St. Anne's playground. Or anywhere else. She was at peace now.

The Worst Kind of Mischief

This happened twenty years ago, in our old cabin in the deep woods of Minnesota, near the bank of Otter Tail Lake. I was ten; my brother Cody was fourteen, and already as tall as a spruce. This is the truest story I've ever told, though I suspect you'll have your doubts. Most folks do. But I was there and saw everything. I'll tell it to you straight, so hold your judgment till I finish.

The night was blacker than pitch. The wind moaned and wailed like a banshee as it tore through the trees. Cody and me, we couldn't sleep. We laid in our beds, staring at the shadows creeping along the ceiling, and listened to our folks talk downstairs. We slept in the loft, see, because our cabin was so small. But at least it was warm, and Ma and Pa were always there.

"Reminds me of the night Jeb Pickering died," said Pa, striking a match. I could smell his sweet pipe tobacco rising through the air.

"Storm was worse that night." Ma's rocking chair creaked. "I know it, because I went out in it."

Cody and I crept up close to the edge of the loft, careful not to make a sound. We held our breaths as we listened.

"You always had a sweet spot for Jeb," said Pa, chuckling softly to himself.

"Says who? I just didn't want to see nothin' happen to him. But the fool took a dare for a few gold pieces and went up yonder to Jackknife Hill. Everyone knows it's a cursed place. Ain't no souls at peace in that old cemetery, least of all Billy Herschel."

"The scoundrel and horse thief who died in a knife fight some years back," Pa recollected.

"Yes sir, that's him. They say there's a curse on his grave, and if you walk on it, he'll reach up and *grab ya*!"

I almost cried out. My whole body was trembling. In my head, I saw a freshly dug grave and a man's skeletal hand reaching out from it, grabbing ahold of my leg. He was pulling and twisting me down. I had to clamp a hand over my mouth to keep from screaming.

Cody saw me trembling and shot me a hard look: *Be quiet, they'll hear you!*

"But Jeb, he went anyway," Ma continued, "for the gold. He had to plunge his jackknife into Billy Herschel's grave. When he didn't return, a bunch of us went on up there to see what had happened. That's when we found him. Or at least his coat, anyway. Nothing was left of poor Jeb, 'cept his knife in the ground. No blood, no bones. It was like the grave just opened up and swallowed him whole."

Ma stopped rocking in the creaky chair, and the only sound in the cabin was the gusty wind beating against the timbers. I glanced at Cody and froze when I saw his expression. He had a distant look as though he were giving heavy consideration to something. Something he shouldn't have been considering at all. Something he should have left well enough alone.

You see, Cody's the type that loves a dare. He never passed up the opportunity to show how brave he was. He'd stick his hand in a hornet's nest just to prove his toughness. I admired Cody, but tonight I was scared for him. I knew exactly what he was thinking. He was going to go up to the old graveyard and challenge the ghost of Billy Herschel, an outlaw who everyone knew did far worse in his lifetime than steal a few nags.

I followed Cody back to bed. "Don't do it," I whispered to him, but it did no good. He merely lay in his bed with a strange kind of smile on his face, gazing up at the ceiling. The supernatural had a hypnotic effect on some people.

The next evening was colder, and the clouds in the west looked red and angry. Cody gathered a bunch of boys from school in the town square and told them Ma's story. He then announced he was going to march up to Jackknife Hill with Pa's Bowie knife and stick it in Billy Herschel's grave, just as Jeb Pickering had done all those years ago. Only he wouldn't die like no coward at the hands of a dead man. He said we could come too, if we weren't too scared to watch, that was.

Several of the boys looked like they'd rather rake muck from a stable, but all of them agreed to go. They had to, if you know what I mean. I went too, but with a heavy heart.

The sky darkened as we made our way to the top of Jackknife Hill. A stampede of thunder clouds rumbled up behind us as we crowded around the crumbling white picket fence bordering the cemetery. We waited along the outside as Cody entered, glancing worriedly at the slanted, bleached-white headstones poking out of the weedy ground like broken teeth. This was the first time I had ever seen fear in his eyes—but it wouldn't be the last.

Slowly, Cody approached Billy Herschel's grave. He pulled the Bowie knife out of his pocket and held it shoulder-high, ready to plunge it into the earth. He took two steps onto Billy's grave and then dropped to one knee. The wind thrashed us like a whip, and lightning tore through the sky. Hesitating for just a moment, Cody jammed the knife into the grave! A sudden explosion of thunder made us all jump. Cody spun around and smiled triumphantly at all of us. Then, his face instantly crumpled in horror as he tried to stand but couldn't! He fell back to the ground, screaming, struggling with some unseen thing around him. And that's when we took off, all of us scrambling back down the hill, running recklessly without stopping till we reached our homes.

"Where's Cody?" Ma demanded as I burst into the cabin. I must have looked like a wind-swept scarecrow standing in the doorway, my pants flecked with mud and my shirt sweat-stained and ripped.

"He … he…" I gasped, but the words wouldn't come. I collapsed into her arms, shaking and sobbing uncontrollably. I had to wait for the tears to pass before I could tell her everything. Pa, listening close by, grabbed his rifle off the wall and stormed out of the house, muttering something about the worst kind of mischief. He was right. We never should have let Cody go through with it. But some folks, they don't see the path they're on and where it's headed until it's too late.

My pa, with the help of a few of the other menfolk, found Cody up there on Jackknife Hill, all right, Pa's Bowie knife stuck in Billy Herschel's grave. And they discovered something else, too. Wasn't Billy Herschel's ghost that done Cody in. It was fear. Fear, when he realized he couldn't get up from the grave. Fear, when he thought he was grabbed by the bony fingers of a dead man. But fear was all it was, because poor Cody had plunged the knife into his own coattails, which the wind had been whipping all around him, and died from shock right on the spot!

I'll always remember Cody and how brave he was, especially on windy nights. And when I get lonely, I head on up to Jackknife Hill and visit his grave where he rests, right next to the infamous horse thief Billy Herschel, who no doubt keeps my brother very good company.

The Secret of Langley Hall

There once lived two sisters who inherited a very fine home upon their parents' death in 1855.

When news arrived of the tragic end of Mr. and Mrs. James Langley, both sisters were devastated. The story they were told was that on their voyage home from England, a storm had struck late at night. Relentless waves battered and capsized their vessel off the coast of Newfoundland, drowning all who were aboard her. The sisters, Catherine and Julia the eldest, fell quickly into a deep and dark depression. They were both socially awkward to begin with and, like their mother, kept mostly to themselves. With their beloved parents gone, the sisters spent every waking moment inside the manor, keeping windows shuttered and doors locked. During this period of mourning, many well-wishers from the nearby towns came to offer their condolences, especially those who knew James Langley well and benefited from his local business dealings.

When the sisters received visitors, they never invited anyone inside. Soon talk spread, as it is apt to do, about their discourteousness. Their father's shipping business was quickly sold for what many considered an absurdly low profit, but who could blame the sisters? They had only just finished their private school studies a few years earlier and knew nothing of the devious transactions of the business world.

When it became apparent that they preferred solitude over the company of friends and neighbors, people stopped visiting and time marched on in its usual gray way. The servants began to quit, even the hardiest and most loyal who'd pledged to help the sisters through this difficult time decided to leave. Eventually, no one was left to cook or clean or monitor the ailing health of the two young women, but over time they adjusted to life in the empty house. To them, the mansion felt more like a mausoleum than a home, its many rooms and passageways filled with the decaying remnants of memories, laughter, and fresh heartache.

Soon after, a dull routine set in for the sisters. The days and months and even the years slipped by in a vast and unbroken void, and eventually a melancholy descended on Julia and Catherine that not even the brightest of summer days could penetrate. With their hearts full of sadness and loss, they even stopped coming to town for food and supplies, and hid themselves away behind locked doors like banished criminals for crimes they did not commit.

For years they were left alone, but curiosity about the sisters and their isolation became too hard to ignore. The local townsfolk whispered of eerie sights and grisly screams coming from the mansion grounds at night. Children slunk around in packs after sunset to catch a glimpse of the house now rumored to be haunted. They hurled rocks at the windows and vandalized statuary in the many gardens around the property. Not only the children but the adults as well believed the old Langley homestead hid its fair share of dark secrets. This fueled the fire for further mischief against the house, until at last it stood as crumbling and foreboding as an old relic from the ancient past.

All the while the sisters watched grimly from their upstairs bedroom window, hoping the unwanted attention would soon wane and their life of uneasy peace could resume. They did not understand why others should fear their eccentricities—or why they should become pariahs in their own community. They simply wanted to be left alone, but that was apparently asking too much.

And so it was with trepidation that Julia and Catherine spied a rider approaching one morning on horseback. He halted at the edge of the expansive front lawn, which by now had become an overgrown field of weeds and wild grass. He gazed fearlessly up at Langley Hall's scarred yet still-impressive façade of cut stone and gothic turrets. The sisters watched with keen interest as he trotted up to the house, dismounted, and gave the front door a hearty knock.

The women shared a brief smile. Then they drifted downstairs to greet their guest.

When they opened the door, they practically swooned. The man had gray, penetrating eyes, a square jaw, and thick hands that bore scars from hard farm labor. He was young, possibly in his twenties, though he carried himself with a maturity one finds with aristocratic breeding or military experience. He wore a long brown overcoat that hung almost to his knees. The sisters were surprised to find it so cold outside. Summer was apparently fading quicker than they'd realized.

Catherine, who had been alone with her sister for so long and secretively yearned for someone new to talk to, immediately invited the handsome stranger inside for tea. Julia frowned at her sister's indiscretion. Their custom was not to invite strangers—or anyone else for that matter—into their home. Yet Julia was also tired of the monotony of their existence. The man, who introduced himself as Peter Blaine and the eldest son of their father's best friend, Lucien, accepted without hesitation.

As he stepped inside the house, he couldn't help but stare with frank disapproval at what he found. The house was indeed falling into similar disrepair on the inside as it was on the out. Cobwebs clung to the corners of every room, a gray patina of dust coated each piece of furniture he saw, and a dull gloom emanated from the very walls themselves, dampening the sunlight and giving the house an aura of abject misery.

The sisters, noting the objection on the young man's face, quickly made apologies. "I'm afraid we've been neglectful of our house work," explained Catherine, stealing a glance at Julia, "but we just haven't felt like ourselves lately."

"Perhaps I can help fix things up," offered Peter, glancing discouragingly at the crumbling stone hearth. "I admit, it may take a while, but my father owes a large debt of gratitude for numerous good deeds that Mr. Langley bestowed upon him before his death. My father is ill these days, I'm afraid, and shudders at the thought of passing away before he can repay the kindnesses. He sent me to help you in any way that I can. I know of your desire for privacy, but if I can be of any service at all—"

"You may," Catherine interrupted, hooking her arm around his and leading him to the back of the house. "Let me show you around. Our house is not as grand as it once was when Mother and Father were alive, but we've kept it up the best we can. We've been so lonely here. Come, let me show you to the kitchen. I'll fix you a nice cup of tea." Julia followed behind.

They sat together for some time and talked, Julia and Catherine listening enthralled to the stories of the outside world. When they inquired about their mansion and what folks were saying about it, Peter frowned and took a long swallow of tea.

"I'm afraid they think it's haunted," he said. "They say there are ghosts all about the property, and they say—oh, I don't mean to give offense—but they say you two are harboring some kind of secret within these walls and that is why you shun the whole community!"

The sisters burst out laughing.

"Ghosts? Here in Langley Hall? How quaint yet perfectly absurd!" Julia exclaimed.

"Why would people say such superstitious things?" Catherine wondered. "If there were ghosts lingering about this place, wouldn't we know?"

"Are there?" Peter's tone became suddenly grave, his expression sharing none of the sisters' mirth.

Julia's laughter cut off quickly as she pushed her empty tea cup aside. "Come," she said, holding out her hand to Peter as she rose from the table. "We will take you on a tour of our home. Langley Hall has seen its share of history, and time can scour the veneer off any fine home. Your assistance in restoring our mansion would be greatly appreciated, and would no doubt settle any old family debts. And perhaps, after you've spent some time here, it would put your mind at ease that its only inhabitants are of the human variety."

They took Peter on a tour of the house, showing him all the rooms except one. The last room on the right of the upper floor was their bedroom, and it was kept locked at all times. There was no discussing the matter.

"We value our privacy very much," explained Catherine. "I hope you respect that while you are here."

Peter nodded, and questioned the matter no further, though his curiosity was undeniably piqued.

When the tour was finished and the projects to be completed were discussed (the sisters insisted on payment for both materials and labor, over Peter's vehement objections), he left the manor and promised to return the next morning to get to work. As they watched him ride off, the sisters felt astounded by their luck. A real man in the house! It had been so long.

As good as his word, Peter returned bright and early the next morning, with a wagon loaded with supplies.

"I'll begin by repairing the masonry around the fireplace," he described, "and then move on to repairing the wainscoting in the parlor and library. I'll repair the windows as soon as the shipment of glass arrives."

The sisters nodded approvingly and retreated to the shadows to watch him work.

Day after day and sometimes well into the night Peter's labors continued, until the house slowly began to shed its gloomy chrysalis. The sisters were pleased to see the restoration unfolding, and were delighted that the pleasant memories of childhood were rejuvenated right along with the house.

For his part, Peter was satisfied with the progress he was making and the improvement to the overall *aura* of the home. When he was finished, perhaps Julia and Catherine would open up the manor to visitors and assuage the local townsfolk's fears of otherworldly activities here.

His father asked just that as Peter sat beside his bed one night. Chest heaving and lungs rattling with pneumonia, the old man told his son how he wished he could visit the old house that was once the finest in all of New Hampshire, before he died. Peter told him he had no idea what the sisters' plans were for the home, though he hoped his work would not be in vain.

He updated his father on the progress of his labors, but left out one key detail: his gnawing curiosity about the upstairs bedroom and the strange *uncanniness* he felt about it. While he couldn't say what it was exactly about the sisters that unnerved him, their actions of late were strangely peculiar. They often stood like sentinels at the bottom of the stairs, watching in silence as he worked. Hours would pass and not a single word would be exchanged, either to each other or to him. Later when he looked up, they'd be gone, without a whisper or a footfall on the stairs or in the hall, as if they'd just disappeared. At odd times he'd see one of the sisters standing at a window or passing from one room to the next as if looking for something. Maybe there was a grain of truth to the rumors about Langley Hall; maybe there *was* a secret. But if so, why did they give him such free reign throughout the house?

Peter ignored the sisters' eccentric behavior and told himself to stop thinking foolishly. After all, it was unfair. These two lonely women had been through so much, with their parents dying so young, leaving the two of them to fend for themselves. Who was he to judge? He was raised to keep an open mind about people. Yet he couldn't keep the locked upstairs bedroom out of his thoughts. It weighed on his mind like a chain around his neck.

One day, his curiosity took over. He could no longer ignore the secret room. Then the day came when he could take it no longer. He was working in the library, pretending not to notice the sisters loitering near the staircase, while keeping the women always in his sight. Suddenly they turned and ascended the stairs swiftly, and this was when Peter leaped into action.

Dropping his tools, he hurried over to the stairs, climbing them quickly and carefully, pausing to listen each time one squealed underfoot. He neither saw nor heard any sign of the sisters, except for a door shutting quietly somewhere above. Peter hastened up the stairs, and when he reached the landing, crept down the long corridor of shadows until he reached the last door on the right. Here he stopped, his pulse racing. The silence of Langley Hall loomed heavily around him, as though the house held its breath and waited for his next move. Peter reached for the doorknob, twisted, and to his surprise found it unlocked. The sisters must be inside, and he braced himself for a furious scorning for violating their *sanctum sanctorum*. Peter pushed the door all the way open and carefully stepped inside. Though the window curtains were drawn, a blade of sunlight stabbed through and illuminated the sheer curtain drawn around a large four poster bed. There were two figures lying prone on the bed. Peter approached the sisters, who must have been napping, and brushed the curtain aside. Horror immediately seized his throat.

Julia's and Catherine's bodies were long past decay and were now two decomposed skeletons. Their gray skulls grinned up at Peter. Two empty amber-tinted bottles lay between the bodies, and a word flashed through Peter's mind: *poison*. Screaming, he turned to flee the room but was stopped in his tracks by the sight of Julia and Catherine in the doorway, their arms outstretched and grasping for him. Their spectral forms no longer looked whole and alive to him. Their color had drained to a bloodless pallor, and through their faint luminescence he could see the doorway and the hall beyond.

"How could you do this to us?" Julia wailed, her voice wavering along with the fading human form she clung to. "Why didn't you respect our wishes?"

Peter's jaw dropped open but no words emerged. The sisters drifted closer to him, and in that moment of utter terror his legs would not obey his command to move. Catherine reached out for him, and when her hand passed through Peter's arm it broke the spell over him and he ran. He felt a deep chill cut through his bones as he passed through their vaporous forms and fled the house, leaving all his tools behind, vowing never to return again. He would tell his father he finished ahead of schedule, and Langley Hall was its old immaculate self again. The old man didn't have the strength left to travel anyway, so Peter would never be caught in the lie.

Julia and Catherine watched out their window as the young man galloped away, whipping his steed fiercely for more speed. Perhaps there would be another visitor someday. They so enjoyed Peter's company; more would always be welcome.

In the meantime, there was work to be finished. And all the time in the world to get it done.

The Thing In The Basement

"Do not bury me in a box," she told him on her deathbed, her voice thin and cracking. "I do not like the dark and the cold. Or the thought of worms chewing through my eyes and mold growing in my bones. Promise me you will cremate me when I die, Stan, and scatter my ashes across my family's farm where I grew up. Swear it upon your life."

"I promise."

He'd said it, and at the time he meant it. With all his heart he intended to do the right thing and honor his wife's last request. The following day she died of pneumonia. A few of Nancy's closest relatives made the trip to attend the funeral and pay their respects. But from the moment they saw Stan, they were overly curious about the funeral arrangements.

"Is she to be buried or cremated?" pestered her sister Margaret. She wore a worried look as if Stan's answer carried grave implications. Stan was flustered by the question. He didn't see how it was anyone's business but his own what he did with his wife's body.

Promise me, Stan.

"She is to be buried at Overlook Cemetery in my family's plot," he declared at dinner that night. "It is a fitting place for a Christian soul to rest. And Nancy, as we all know, was a devout member of the church."

This, at least, was a truthful statement. Nancy loved the church as much as he, and devoted countless weekend hours in volunteer work for the pastor. Though he was breaking an oath to his deceased wife, he took comfort in the fact that she would be resting surrounded by family members, whose spirits would escort her lovingly to the other side.

Cremation. How he loathed the very idea.

The body was a temple, the Bible said. Why would anyone want to defile themselves and burn in Perdition's flames? Stan shuddered at the thought of a fire devouring his wife, leaving behind nothing but a small mound of ashes and charred bone. How revolting. It was almost *disrespectful* of her to deny him the opportunity to visit her at her gravesite. He hated himself for lying to her on her deathbed, but with each passing day following the funeral, he felt more at ease, more comfortable with his decision. He was sure he'd done the right thing. And, what's more, he was certain if Nancy were still alive, she would have agreed with his judgment on the matter. *A wife must not separate from her husband.* He'd heard Pastor Roberts say that a dozen times in sermons. If he allowed her dust to be scattered over a cornfield in Nebraska, how would he ever lie beside his love again in eternal rest?

The matter was settled.

When the funeral was over, Stan couldn't wait for Nancy's relatives to go home. Something about them disquieted him. Perhaps it was the way they stared at him throughout the entire ceremony, as though he were somehow responsible for her death. Margaret in particular scowled fiercely when Nancy's coffin was lowered into the earth. She approached Stan in private after the funeral to tell him he would be sorry for violating her trust and burying her.

"I know my own sister," she spat at him. "This is not what she wanted."

"It will be fine," he replied softly. *Especially when you and your clan go back home,* he almost added.

Margaret turned away and strode off briskly to rejoin her family, when suddenly she stopped and regarded the heavy, rain-swollen clouds with intense scrutiny. "I smell a storm coming," she said, apparently to no one in particular. "It will make the ground soft."

Stan shivered in a stiff breeze.

There was a proper but thankfully short gathering at his home after the funeral. People appeared to be in a hurry to leave Stan's house, which suited him just fine. To tell the truth, he was looking forward to some peace and quiet. To think things over, plan for the future. A future without Nancy, a woman he'd been married to for forty years.

For the next three days Stan adjusted to life as a widower. He went about his routines, completing day to day tasks, though more than once he had the alarming sensation of somebody watching over his shoulder. *Nonsense*, he thought. *I'm just letting Margaret spook me.* And there was no way he was letting that old crone get under his skin.

At night Stan would settle into his easy chair in the study, tossing and turning. The silence of the house was a curious thing, resonating with a lifetime of love and pain and laughter, a million tiny whispers his ears strained to hear but could not quite capture. And then there was the rain. Since the night of the funeral, it had rained almost relentlessly. At its heaviest moments, it buried the silence of the empty house under the staccato fury of charging bulls.

One night, Stan listened to this discordant melody until his eyes grew heavy and his head sank forward. Then a sudden noise in the house startled him awake.

The sound, he was certain, had come from below him in the basement. Stan glanced at the wall clock during the next stutter of lightning and was surprised to find he'd been asleep for hours. The rain was still beating down

(*It will make the ground soft*)

with relentless fervor, and the house was in complete darkness. The power must have gone out. Stan called out to Nancy to be sure she was all right, and for a moment he was puzzled when he didn't receive a response. Then he remembered he was alone now, and shook his head at his own foolishness. *I must be getting old if I can't remember burying my own wife.*

The noise came again. A hollow metallic clang and the scrape of something heavy. Below him.

In the basement.

Stan sat up alertly now, wiping sweat away from his eyes. *What is down there making that noise?*

He needed to investigate.

He was not going to call the police and look like a fool if it turned out to be an animal of some sort trapped down there. He hadn't gone downstairs in over a year now. Ever since they moved the washer and dryer upstairs, there'd been no reason to go in the basement. It was an insufferably damp, moldy place. Nancy always hated it. On rainy days, the basement floor soaked up water like a sponge. It also reeked of mold and mildew, which grew in furry black tentacles up the walls. He meant to take care of the stains a long time ago, but other matters arose and he forgot about it. Now he dreaded seeing what had become of his home's subterranean chamber.

Sighing, Stan trudged to the basement.

He wore a pair of slippers, jeans, and a T-shirt. It had been warm that morning, an unseasonably mild day for late October. But when he opened the door and peered down into the gloom waiting for him there, he was struck by a draft so icy and foul it made him shut the door at once and run to a window for fresh air.

Something is wrong down there, he thought. *It may not be clean, but basements and cellars shouldn't smell like* that. *It smelled like something died down there, maybe a whole lot of somethings, rotting in their own juices.*

After the stink faded, Stan turned to face the basement once again. He tried to turn on the light but nothing happened. *Power must be out all over the house.* He reached for his emergency flashlight clipped on the wall and shined it down the black throat of the stairwell. He was shocked at what reflected back at him. Water. Lapping gently over the bottom two steps. Then, in his flashlight beam, he caught a flicker of movement. It happened quickly, so quick he wasn't sure he could believe his eyes. He blinked and rubbed his eyes and waited for a few more seconds for it to reappear.

Then, from somewhere else in the basement, he heard the faint sound of splashing.

Stan kept the flashlight beam focused on the choppy water. Why was it choppy? What could possibly be swimming around down there? He was terrified of the thought of a family of disgusting vermin nesting in his basement. Could rats swim? He had no idea.

As much as he wanted to close the door and board it up forever, he couldn't ignore the problem down there any longer. Eventually a house with a bad foundation will develop other problems. He would have to fix whatever was going on down there, which meant he must inspect the problem.

Taking a deep breath, Stan gathered his courage and descended the stairs.

When he reached the bottom, he slowly waved the flashlight's beam back and forth over the water as he looked for any sign of movement, rat or otherwise.

Nothing broke the surface. As far as the feeble beam could discern, nothing swam in its murky depths, either.

Stan took a few more steps down and stopped just above the water line. By leaning forward and holding onto the railing with one hand, he was able to scan the rest of the basement with his flashlight. Large cracks in the concrete block walls were oozing an astonishing amount of water. The angular skeletal arm of the out-matched sump pump sat cold and silent in the far corner.

That's what I must have heard, he thought. When it overloaded and died, it must have made a sound and woke me up.

Suddenly, something fast and sleek shot across the inky water.

A blade of horror stabbed his heart. Stan jerked back from the shapeless thing, and his glasses slipped off his nose! They clattered on the last dry step and bounced into the water, quickly disappearing.

Terror rushed through him in a nauseous wave. He had to get his glasses back, *had* to, but stick his hand in that water? No way! But what other choice did he have? He could see no better than a mole without them. And his second pair broke a long time ago.

Exhaling in frustration, he stuck his hand in the icy water and felt around for the glasses. He thought of a time when he was a kid and was once dared to stick his hand in the gaping hole of a diseased tree trunk. He flaunted the odds back then, believing that nothing coiled inside was going to strike him, and he flaunted those same beliefs now.

Nothing.

He could search faster if he used both hands. Stan put the flashlight between his teeth and let go of the railing. He stepped down into the water, which rose to the middle of his calves. Dirt, silt, and grainy material—probably dissolved concrete—swept through his fingers. Then, when he was about to give up, his hand closed around something.

Success! He recognized the feel of his glasses' metal frames and yanked them out of the water. At the exact moment he pulled them out, something smooth and fleshy seized his wrist and tried to wrest the glasses from his hand.

"Give them back!" he screamed, flailing his other arm at whatever the thing was. He was practically blind, and all he could make out was a vague shape of something human-like, but he couldn't be sure. He threw a punch and his fist brushed against the thing's outer coat of slime. A garbled cry and a ferocious stink assaulted his senses. The thing released his glasses and Stan quickly slid them onto his face. As his eyes adjusted and his sight returned, he quickly wished he never put those glasses back on. He should have let the unknown thing keep them as a trophy.

The thing had a lumpish head and a long, rippled body of gray, rotting flesh. It sucked, gurgled and glared at him through two slitted black eyes. A row of blackened teeth lined the inside of its gnashing mouth. Stan held his hands out in self-defense, his heart pounding a hole through his chest. With a grunt, the thing pitched itself forward and sank those sickening teeth into his wrist. Stan shrieked as blistering pain burned through his arm and up into his shoulder. The thing released him a moment later and flipped backward into the water.

Stan turned away and raced back up the stairs into the safety of his kitchen and the comfort of daylight, cradling his wrist as he sobbed in pain and shock. Two rows of puncture marks beaded with blood.

"Why is this happening to me?" he cried to the empty room.

Because you didn't listen, came a harsh response. Stan knew he was alone, but the voice he heard sounded exactly like Nancy's.

After wrapping his wrist in bandages, Stan scrambled for a kitchen chair and jammed it under the doorknob, backing away slowly like a man who'd trapped a dangerous and cunning animal.

He ran upstairs to his bedroom to pack a suitcase. He was getting out of here. Stan and Nancy never had any children of their own, but he could call Margaret for a place to stay. He would apologize for being so thick-headed and not honoring his wife's dying wishes.

He dialed the number, his hand trembling so badly he almost couldn't punch the buttons. When Margaret answered on the second ring, he blurted, "You have to help me, Margaret! I need to come stay with you. It's horrible … the thing downstairs … Nancy … you were right…"

"Slow *down*, Stan," she interrupted. "You aren't making any sense at all."

Stan took a deep breath. He flung shirts and jeans into a suitcase, dumped his toothbrush, razor, and comb in after them.

"I have to get out now! She's back. She's downstairs! Oh, it's horrible, Margaret. You were right. I should have listened to her."

A long silence seeped through the phone, and just as Stan was about to ask if she was still there, he heard, "So Nancy isn't resting very well, is she, Stan?"

A series of crashing blows thundered through the house. Stan squeezed the phone painfully. "Oh my God. I have to get out of here."

"'Pride cometh before the fall.' Isn't that right? Proverbs 16:18, I believe?"

Wood groaned and splintered. The sound of something wet and lumpy thudded on the kitchen floor.

"You were the one who chose to bury her in Overlook Cemetery as the rain poured down and the mud formed, so you can put her *back* yourself, Stan."

A kitchen chair knocked over. A table leg scraped the linoleum floor.

Stan dropped the phone. His wrist ached terribly. Blood flowed out from the edges of the bandages, and he had never felt as tired before as he did just then. So tired and alone. Stan slumped to the floor. His last clear thought was of Nancy on their wedding day, Nancy and the beautiful smile she gave him when he slipped the ring over her finger. Nancy and her little white teeth.

"Margaret?" he croaked, gasping for air. "I never believed in ghosts or monsters or anything like that before."

A dry chuckle echoed over the phone. "You have surprisingly little faith for a man who's spent so much time in church."

The Nancy-thing snickered, thumping up the stairs.

Halloween Night

It is Halloween night.
Can you feel it in the air?
A light autumn breeze
And a creak on the stair.
A house cold and empty
Without light nor a sound,
But the whispers of voices
When nobody's around.
The darkness within
Stirs with its hosts,
Breezes and cold spots
And signs of the ghosts.
You sense them around you

Playing tricks with your hair;
A cold breath on your neck
And you know they are there.

Pass this house quickly
If you are lost in the night,
One glance through a window
May give you a fright.
Many travelers have sought
Refuge through its door;
Many travelers have not
Been seen anymore.

It is Halloween night
With a change in the air.
A shivery feeling
Of eyes everywhere
Get away from the house
Put it out of your sight!
Abandon it forever
To the specters of night.

The Wind Breathes Cold

Martin Hilliard eased his car over to the side of the road and cut the engine. He listened to his breathing in the stillness, a ragged sound reminding him he wasn't getting any younger, and the years were slipping by quickly. He stared through the smudged glass at the narrow dirt path twisting and disappearing into the shadowy blue woods. Dry wind strummed the trees. The chattering leaves sounded like teeth.

He stepped out of the car, stretched his sore back. He'd driven all night to find the house again.

The closer he got, the worse the sky became. And now his mood matched the darkness of the clouds.

Why did I even bother to come back? he wondered, and not for the first time on this journey. The answer repeated itself for at least the hundredth time: *Because you had to. Because some things don't want to be forgotten.*

Shaking his head, he started down the threaded path into the cool interior of the woods. Mosquitoes whined in his ears, landing every few seconds on his sweaty face. He waved and swatted them away. He gulped air, feeling at any moment like he might faint. He really needed to exercise more. He shouldn't be getting tired so quickly, especially with so little exertion.

He stopped and leaned his considerable bulk against the trunk of a massive tree. For one anxious moment he felt a surge of panic ripple through him, and he fought the urge to return to his car. Then the wind shifted and changed, exhaling a breath so cold it made his skin ripple with gooseflesh. There was indeed something amiss about this desolate place. A fog sat like a heavy pall over everything. In its stillness he could almost hear whispered voices calling his name.

But he continued on. The trail he followed led through brush and pines to a house that sulked like a scorned child in the gloomy woods. All he could think about was what lay buried in the back, and how urgent it had suddenly become to rest a palm against the cold, unbroken surface of the grave. Only then could he be assured its occupant hadn't risen to haunt the living.

But what if it had, Martin? What will you do if you get there and find the grave is empty?

He wished his anxiety, which had become a part of his life like a shadow he couldn't dodge, would go away.

Coming back was supposed to be good for him, wasn't it? Isn't that what his doctor told him; what *all* good doctors said? To overcome your fears, you have to confront them, so you can take charge of your own emotions again. Since the day of the accident twenty years ago, Martin felt the eerie presence of something dark and formidable and *hungry* trying to get his attention, a thing of almost physical substance twisting his insides and making his days a living nightmare. His doctor told him he was suffering from an extreme case of unwarranted guilt, and that he had to come to terms with it. To see it for what it was: a shade of the past, powerless except for whatever influence his mind allowed it to have over him. Martin was tired. He didn't want to see the old house in the woods, but he knew he had no choice. Something there was waiting for him. He felt certain he could get answers if he was open to receiving them, but what exactly those answers were, he couldn't say.

You know. You've never forgotten Toby, and what happened that day. You ran ... but it has always been one step behind you.

Martin did indeed feel Toby's presence in these woods. The sensation of being watched stole over him. He could feel the air thickening with an approaching storm. In response, his chest tightened painfully, and his lungs worked harder than ever to supply oxygen to his weary body. Without warning, the image of the frail twelve-year-old boy appeared in his mind. Toby.

With clumps of thinning hair on a huge, misshapen head. Toby and his frighteningly dark eyes, studying him closely every night in his dreams, like those of a thief glaring covetously at a prize. What *was* the prize? His soul? Martin wasn't going to give it to him, even though he probably owed Toby so much more.

A victim of cruel mistreatment by other children, Toby never attended school or church, and spent his days instead sitting in his dismal house with his sallow-skinned mother looking out for his needs. Sitting and watching out his smeared little window as the days, months, and years drifted by. If it wasn't for Martin, he would have had no friends to play with at all.

Up ahead, Martin heard the sound of twigs snapping, followed by mischievous laughter. He followed the rest of the path until he emerged in a small clearing littered with pine needles and patches of brown grass. In the middle of the clearing sat the house, a simple structure so beaten down by weather and neglect that it leaned slightly to one side, as though the burden of its own existence was too much to bear. Most of the windows were smashed. The white paint was washed down to a dull gray.

As he stared across the clearing, he saw two boys standing in front of the house, chucking rocks at it. Most of the rocks thunked off the roof and landed harmlessly on the ground. This shouldn't have bothered Martin so, but his heart was racing and sweat broke out across his face. This is crazy, he thought. Why should I be so afraid of these children? It wasn't witnessing the vandalism of private property that unnerved him; it was being back here that was causing his anxiety to spring to life like a wild thing rattling its cage.

Led by a strong yet inexplicable compulsion, Martin rushed over and shouted to the boys to stop. At the sound of Martin's voice, which to his own ears sounded nearly hysterical, the boys scampered away. They crashed into the woods and disappeared before Martin could even get a good look at them.

He almost called out to apologize to them. The old house was clearly abandoned and had been since the fire twenty years ago. Why did it matter if a couple of kids pitched rocks at it? It didn't, but Martin suddenly felt protective of the property, as though it belonged somehow to him.

When the echoes of hasty retreat and laughing voices faded from the forest, Martin circled around to the back of the house. He found the sunken grave set back about fifty feet from the house. A wooden cross crudely fashioned by two planks nailed together and reinforced with leather straps stood at the head of the grave. A pauper's grave, he thought sadly, the only thing poor Toby's mother could afford. The cross didn't appear very old, however, and he wondered if somebody was coming back regularly to tend to the grave. Or pay their respects.

Martin knelt and studied the simple grave for a moment, the slight oblong dent in the ground. Oddly, nothing grew on it. The weeds and grass seemed to avoid the area completely. He was actually stunned nobody had dug the grave up by now, to see what a deformed skeleton might look like. No doubt it was superstition that kept most of the vandals away. When Martin was a kid and came to the woods to play with

Toby, people were already gossiping about the place. Some of his own friends at school looked at him funny or shunned him from their activities. For that he blamed Toby, but he shouldn't have. He saw that now. Toby was not the reason why people used to look down on him. It was their own blind prejudice and hatred of differences, but at the time, Martin didn't see it that way. If he were to be honest with himself, there was probably nobody he hated more than Toby back then.

In the distance, a trembling grind of thunder. Martin stood and looked at the dilapidated house. An electric current of energy climbed up the back of his legs. Goosebumps popped out on his arms. He was not a religious man but he made the sign of the cross anyway, though he took no comfort from the gesture. Why should he be feeling this way, so guilty for a freak accident, so *haunted*? He had been only thirteen! What thirteen-year-old knew what he was doing?

Come inside, Marty. I've been keeping this miserable old place standing just for you. Now we can play forever.

After another crack of thunder, a torrent of rain started falling. He was too far from the car to bother going back, so instead he bounded inside the house, surprised to find the back door unlocked, as if somebody really had been expecting him.

Actually, from the looks of the place, it was doubtful anyone had been inside the old house for years. The house had been left on its own too long and was now rotting away. Most of the plaster walls were buckling from moisture damage and, in some places, turning unusual shades of yellow and gray. Martin knew he could probably push his thumb right through parts of the wall if he tried, but the house overall seemed sturdy enough for one more visitor. Especially one who wasn't staying long. As his doctor advised, he was facing his demons. But nobody told him how long he had to stay. Once the rain subsided, he would go back to his car and put as many miles between himself and this godforsaken place as he could. And good riddance to it all.

In the meantime, he explored the creaky darkness.

In the living room, the withered husks of brown, yellow and scarlet leaves blew in through the shattered window and lay in heaps around the floor, the litter of countless autumns. Martin wandered around the room, listening to the mournful wind whistle through the cracks and crevices of the walls.

Strangely, the air felt at least twenty degrees cooler *inside*, and a chill ran down his back. The blackest shadows he'd ever seen seeped down the walls and pooled in every corner of the house. He left the living room and found an old lantern on a shelf in the kitchen, and a sodden box of matches in a drawer. It took him five attempts to find one dry enough to burn.

The glow from the lantern cast his face in an eerie sheen. He almost didn't recognize himself as he passed by a mirror. I've become one of them, he thought. A murderer who comes back to the spot of his damnation, reliving his victim's torment all over again.

He pushed the depressing thought out of his mind and, holding the lantern out in front of him, started up a set of stairs into the darkness waiting for him above.

He moved with purpose, though what that purpose was he didn't know. He stopped at the threshold of one of the upstairs bedrooms. Sheets of rain slanted in through the broken window. Black scorch marks fanned out like raven's wings on the wall across from him. On the threadbare carpet lay a dark stain that he couldn't take his eyes off of. Feeling a mixture of revulsion and curiosity, he started moving toward it, unaware of what he was doing. His mind was clouding again, and his thoughts were returning to the past.

Play toy soldiers with me, Marty.

He always hated playing toy soldiers with Toby. It was a child's game, and he couldn't understand why any boy his age—even Toby—would want to waste countless hours amassing armies of plastic figurines and strategically positioning them for battle. Toby would even make grunting noises when he put his soldiers through maneuvers, and growl like an engine when a pretend tank rolled onto the battlefield.

Toby's mother was their housekeeper, and he knew his own mother had a soft spot for her and her special needs son. Still, why did she have to rent his friendship out without ever asking how he felt about it? He always wished she would come and rescue him on these boring afternoons, but she never did; she'd sometimes even leave him there the whole day to play with Toby, never bothering to check on him and ask him if he was having fun. He started to have bad thoughts—*terrible* thoughts, really—about Toby, like how to make him hate Martin so he wouldn't want him to come over again. One day Martin started stealing Toby's favorite soldiers, or breaking them when he wasn't looking. Toby would bawl like a baby when he found his general without a head or a tank missing a wheel. Martin couldn't help laughing when the awkward boy's chest heaved and made its little hiccup noises. Martin didn't enjoy doing these things to Toby, but it was necessary because his mother just wouldn't listen to him.

The wind whooshed into the empty room, bringing him back to the present. Martin stared at the dark spot on the floor and heard a ringing vibration in his ears. The electrical current he felt outside was back, this time originating in his head and sliding down the back of his neck. The unmistakable feeling of being watched returned too, and he glanced back down the hall to make sure he was alone.

I forgive you, Marty. Come inside and let's play soldiers. I'll let you be a general. You can even keep your head on, my old friend.

Martin shuddered.

He stepped inside the room involuntarily and stood in front of that spot where Toby had died long ago. Where he had burned. The memories overwhelmed him in a storm of violently edited images: Toby, crouched on the floor with an array of green army guys in front of him, as though protecting their beloved leader from something; a goofy grin on his pimply face as he waved Martin into his room; two candles burning low on a short table next to him. He remembered it had been late in the day, and soon the little house without any electricity would be in total darkness. The shadows from the candles danced on the wall. Toby's own shadow was a disfigured wraith lunging and jumping over and over as the candle flames sputtered.

"Play with me, Marty," said Toby in a little four- year-old's voice. "Why are you just standing there? Don't you want to be a general?"

Martin fumed. He'd had it. He decided to tell his mother he wasn't going to stay—that he'd *walk* the ten miles back to their house if he had to—but he was not going to play with Toby any longer.

As he turned to go, Toby stood up in protest, knocking the candles off the table. From out in the hallway Martin heard a *whooshing* sound, and smelled the curtains burning. Next, Toby started screaming. "Help me, Marty!" he cried, but Martin didn't move. He remained in the darkening hallway, orange light shimmering behind him. A tear slipped down his cheek. Toby screamed, and Martin heard a thump as something heavy struck the floor. Then Toby's mother came bounding up the stairs, shooting past him and into the room. The rest of the memory after that was a blur. As the visions began to fade and the screams died away into whispers, Martin found himself crouched in the spot where Toby had been, next to the window, hugging himself while tears streamed down his face.

"I'm so sorry, Toby," he sobbed. All his anguish let go at once, and he mourned for Toby, a child whose life was cut short by Martin's own petty selfishness. When he opened his eyes again and dried them, he noticed the first long shadows of twilight slipping into the room. And he noticed something else, too. Across from him on the floor sat a little green toy soldier, plastic semi-automatic pointed right at his chest. Martin stood and inspected the toy, turning it over and over in his hands, wondering how it got there.

"Want to play toy soldiers, Marty?"

The voice made him jump, and the lantern slipped from his hand and crashed to the floor. Flames exploded and fanned greedily along the old carpet and up onto the walls with surreal speed, bursting into a fiery lotus of red heat. In the middle of the conflagration stood Toby, as whole and alive as the last time Martin saw him, the surface of his black and depthless eyes reflecting the flickering orange and red light.

"Play with me, Marty." He held his arms open, beckoning him to come. Billows of black smoke wreathed Toby's head. "Why don't you play with me? We can have such great fun!"

Martin lunged for the door before the smoky haze could choke off the remaining breathable air, and bolted down the stairs.

Staggering outside, he fell to his knees, spluttering and coughing. The rain had stopped and blue shadows seeped out of the forest. Phantoms of slate-colored smoke drifted from the windows of the house.

Forcing his exhausted legs to obey, he got up but stumbled backwards, tripping on a protruding root. His head struck the ground, and for a moment everything went black. When he regained his vision, he saw fire crackling in every room of the house. Soon the whole structure would collapse on itself. Kicking his legs in the mud, he managed to pull himself up and put some distance between himself and the house. But it was not enough. A bolt of fire exploded out of Toby's window, sailed over the porch in a spray of sparks, and struck Martin as he ran. As he crumpled to the ground he had a vision of being on a battlefield, of soldiers in green uniforms rushing past him. One stopped and hooked an arm under Martin's shoulder, helping him up. The soldier led him deeper into the woods, where explosions and gunshots rang out in the darkness. The war, Martin feared, was only just beginning.

The soldiers could run on forever.

The Midnight Road

The silvery mist appeared out of nowhere, shrouding the desolate country road and turning the night air cold and damp. Taylor Murphy switched the windshield wipers on, the high beams off, and rolled up the window. Clenching the steering wheel until her knuckles turned white, she told herself it was better to take it slow and get back to her hotel room late than run the Volkswagen into a ditch or wrap it around a tree.

This strange and roiling fog was the only blemish on an otherwise beautiful summer evening. An evening filled with love, romance, music and dancing.

Her sister's wedding replayed over and over in Taylor's mind. The quaint church with its nineteenth-century architecture, the elegant reception hall, the delicious food—all of it had been picturesque and ripped from the pages of every girl's fantasy wedding.

Of course her sister deserved a long and happy life with her beau, and Taylor was very happy that she'd found the right man. But privately she bristled all the way through the ceremony as she stood by her sister's side as the maid of honor. *Don't I deserve a little happiness, too?* Taylor thought to herself. Love seemed determined to elude her. Lauren had met her future husband on the first day of a new job, and knew at once that he was the one. Taylor believed fate held similar plans for her, but so far the wait had been long and torturous.

Just get it over with, she thought dismally. *If I'm to die alone and childless, then let it happen fast. Don't make me suffer any longer.*

She felt guilty for thinking such a horrible thought—on her sister's wedding day no less!—but Taylor was thirty-eight and not getting any younger.

Through the milky haze she could make out the bent and knotted shapes of trees, like curious skeletons crowding over her for a closer look. She turned the radio on for company, but all she found was bouncy pop, screeching rock, and bittersweet classical music. Nothing that could lift her mood. Sighing, she switched the radio off and listened to the silence instead. At least it played a tune she recognized: melancholy. And that suited her just fine for the moment. Especially in this fog. Fog so thick it actually constricted her breathing.

As she considered pulling over and calling for help, a rift opened in the gloom. She could again see the road and the trees—which looked innocent enough without the ominous mist and her overactive imagination—and above it all, a few winking stars.

And she saw something else coming up fast in her headlights. Someone walking down the middle of the road, where nobody had any business being, especially in the dead of night. Taylor slowed the car for a better look.

To her astonishment, it was a young woman in a flowing white dress, her long blond hair swept back in a black headband. She was heading in the other direction, but she turned to look at Taylor as she passed.

Her dress, Taylor thought with a chill. *It shines.*

It was not the sort of thing you'd expect to see someone wearing on a night like this. For one, it was long and elegant, with matching white gloves and white ballroom shoes. She wore no coat, and must have been chilled to the bone. No, she was surely not dressed for a stroll down a gravelly country lane.

Concerned, Taylor brought the car to a stop and rolled down the passenger side window. "Excuse me!" she called. "Are you all right? Do you need a lift?"

It was an idiotic question. Anyone walking around out here in the middle of the night needed help, didn't they? Her car must have broken down somewhere up the road, her cell phone batteries were dead, and she was looking for the nearest service station. But if that was the case, why was she ignoring Taylor and walking away?

"Wait!" She put the car in reverse. "Let me give you a ride home or something!"

A cool breeze clawed at the woman's long blond hair as she turned around. "You don't have to do this," she said in a flat, weirdly monotone voice. "You're still able to make a choice."

Taylor frowned. She had no idea what that meant. "It won't be morning for several hours," she told the stranger. "You'll freeze out here without a jacket. You shouldn't be alone on the road, anyway. Hop in, I'll take you wherever you want to go."

With obvious reluctance, the mysterious woman opened the door and got in, a breath of frosty air rushing in after her.

"I'm Taylor," she said, offering her hand. Her passenger ignored it. Taylor stared at her, probably longer than she should have, trying to figure out if she was ill or intoxicated or something else. Her behavior was certainly odd. At first glance she appeared quite young, possibly eighteen or nineteen, but her sallow skin and grief-stricken eyes belonged to a person much older, someone who was no stranger to pain and sorrow. Taylor found it difficult to pry her eyes away.

"I'm sorry," she said awkwardly, shaking her head. "I know it's not polite to stare."

"Don't worry about it." The lady in white kept her eyes straight ahead and focused on the road. "There's not a lot that bothers me anymore."

Taylor turned the car around and drove back the way she came. After a few minutes of silence, she said, "I can't believe this," waving her hand at the mist, "I've never seen anything like it before."

"It comes and it goes," replied the young woman wistfully. "Sometimes it never comes at all."

Taylor found the enigmatic answer a bit too disquieting. Perhaps the woman wasn't drunk or ill after all; maybe she was delusional. It might explain her weird mannerisms and the blank, almost hypnotic expression she wore as she stared into the mist.

"I never caught your name," said Taylor.

"Hmm?"

"Your name. You didn't tell me."

The woman sighed. "Annabel Young."

"Nice to meet you, Miss Young. Where are you headed to this evening?"

"I was on my way to see my boyfriend, Stephen. He's the one, you know. I feel it deep inside. I could *never* live without him. He's taking me to my sister's wedding, you see, but my car broke down back where you found me. I was walking to get help when—"

"Your sister's wedding?" Taylor interrupted, a strange feeling creeping over her. "How funny is that? I was at my sister's wedding today, too!"

The woman acted as though she didn't hear her and kept right on talking. "—when you came along. You weren't supposed to, though. That's not how it works. Where did you come from? How did you get here?" A shadow lurked behind the stranger's eyes, as if a dark thought had entered her mind.

"What do you mean?" she asked.

The hitchhiker suddenly grabbed Taylor's right hand off the steering wheel, turned it over, and examined her palm closely. Taylor almost lost control of the car. It swerved into the oncoming lane, coming dangerously close to crashing into the ditch, as Taylor fought the wheel with her left hand. In the headlights the mist swarmed like a boiling cauldron, stirred up by the vehicle's sudden violent motion. Taylor jerked her hand away from Annabel and straightened the car out.

"What did you do that for?" she exclaimed, her heart hammering wildly. "You want to get us both killed?"

"I needed to know."

"Know *what?*"

"If you were the one."

Taylor laughed. She didn't mean to, but with each passing second it was becoming more and more obvious that something was wrong with Annabel. Deeply wrong.

Maybe you should just pull over and let her out before she pulls another crazy stunt like that, nagged her instincts. Perhaps it *was* a mistake to pick up this hitchhiker. Taylor considered returning Annabel to her car and calling for the police or a taxi driver to come pick her up, but then thought better of it. Who knew how long it would be before someone arrived? In this weather, Annabel could catch her death wearing nothing more than a dress. She needed to just hurry up and drop Annabel off safely at her boyfriend's house and say good riddance to her once and for all.

She sighed miserably and rubbed the back of her neck. For a day that had started off so enchanting, it was turning out to be quite a nuisance!

"How much farther?" Taylor asked, not caring if she sounded rude.

"His house is just a little bit up the road." Annabel glanced over at Taylor. "I'm sorry. I shouldn't have touched you like that."

"Forget about it."

"No, really, I don't want you to hate me. You're a good person, I can see that. I think he might be the one you've been waiting for."

Taylor felt a wave of pins and needles flood through her body. "What do you mean by that, Annabel? You're scaring me."

But Annabel declined to answer. She sat back in her seat silently as the car cruised through the mist.

Taylor felt the tension in her neck claw its way up to her head. The voice urgently nagged her again to stop the car and let her passenger out at once.

You don't know who she is, she could be carrying a weapon, and she's obviously crazy. Why are you still helping her?

Good question. She couldn't explain it if she had to, but from the moment she laid eyes on Annabel, she had a hunch she knew her from somewhere. Call it intuition. Although in the past her intuition had led her into some embarrassingly bad relationships with men, this time she had confidence in her feelings. She just couldn't let Annabel go just yet. She had to see where this road they were on led to.

Taylor drove for several more minutes in silence, scanning the road for any sign of a driveway, a mailbox, or a light that might indicate a house up ahead. Finally the peculiar mist thinned and a pair of dim porch lights on an old white farmhouse shined up ahead. Patches of wispy fog scudded past its windows.

"Well, looks like we're in luck," Taylor said, relieved. She brought the car to a stop in front of the house and turned to look at her passenger. "This must be Stephen's pla—"

She froze.

A scream rose in her throat.

The lady in white had disappeared.

Taylor twisted around in her seat, but the backseat was empty, too. There was no way she just opened her door and got out without Taylor noticing. She just … *vanished*. Like a ghost. Here one minute, gone the next. Taylor closed her eyes, her heart thundering, and told herself to calm down and catch her breath. Should she just drive away and chalk the whole experience up to exhaustion and too much drinking at the reception? But she'd only had one glass of wine, and that was over three hours ago! And she was not tired. In fact, since picking up Annabel, her nerves had been wired and anxious, as if some part of her was waiting for something crazy like this to happen.

As if some part of her knew all along that it would.

What did all of this mean then?

One thing was certain: Annabel, whomever she was—*whatever* she was—had been in the car with her, and that was not a figment of her imagination.

Taylor never believed in ghosts before, but there was no other logical explanation. And then there was the mist. As though connected somehow to Annabel's presence on the road, the mist shredded into steamy white filaments and began to drift apart. Through a hole in the heavy cloud cover, a round pearl moon gleamed down on the house.

She was about to drive off—putting as many miles as she could between herself and the house—when a man stepped out onto the porch carrying a flashlight.

"Can I help you?" he called, shining the light on her car. She recognized the voice immediately, even though she'd never met the man before. *Stephen.* She felt certain it was him, and a shuddering urge to talk to him overtook her. Where did this unexpected longing come from?

Maybe when Annabel touched my hand she left a little piece of herself inside me. A part of her soul, or perhaps a lingering desire for her old love.

Lowering her window, she watched the man approach her car. In the hazy moonlight, his face looked earnest and handsome.

"I'm Taylor," she said, remaining in the car. "Sorry for bothering you so late, but I just had something very weird happen to me, and I was wondering—I know how this is going to sound—but I was hoping you might be able to give me some answers."

He smiled warmly. "My name's Stephen. It's a bad night to be out here driving alone. The fog is thicker than pea soup today."

"Breaking up a little now finally." She offered a smile of her own. "Is it always this bad around here at night?"

Stephen glanced up and down the road and shrugged. "Not really. It comes and it goes, depending on the night."

Taylor felt the prickly hot sensation of *déjà vu* wash over her.

"You okay?" he asked. "Want to come in out of the cold? Maybe I can give you those answers you wanted. At the very least, I can fix you a warm cup of coffee."

With her instincts oddly silent on the subject of going into a strange man's house alone in the middle of the night, Taylor followed Stephen inside and sat at the kitchen table. She expected an interior monologue, usually in her stern mother's voice, about the dangers of trusting men she'd just met.

But Stephen put her thoughts and fears at ease. How, she didn't know. Did it even matter?

Taylor enjoyed the warmth of the house as she sipped the coffee Stephen gave her. "What is it that you want to know, Taylor?" he asked.

She told him the events of the day, starting with Lauren's wedding and ending with Annabel disappearing next to her in the car. When she was finished, she waited for Stephen's response, but he remained quiet and pensive for a long time, staring into his coffee cup. When he finally spoke, his voice trembled.

"I'll be right back," he said, wandering out of the room and returning a few seconds later with a framed photograph. "I was in love with her. Annabel Maria Young, prom queen and valedictorian at Westmont High. One night in June, 1994, we were planning on going to a party at a friend's house. Normally I would've driven us, but my Camaro had blown a gasket the previous night and was in the shop. Annabel was coming to pick me up, but it was a misty night, much like this one. That's when it happened. She lost control of the car and it struck a tree. Just like that. Her future, *our* future, gone in an instant. I was devastated. The life we'd dreamed up for each other was never going to happen. Somehow, I knew it was all my fault."

"No, it wasn't, Stephen." Taylor reached across the table and grasped his hands tightly. He glanced at them quizzically for a moment, then gently turned them over, staring at her palms.

"You said she looked at your palm?" he asked.

Taylor nodded. "It almost got us killed!" *Or at least one of us*, she almost added.

Stephen stood up from the table and started pacing the floor. "Annabel always claimed to be able to read palms. She fancied herself something of a psychic, I guess." He said it was a grin, but Taylor could tell that part of him believed it.

"I wonder what she saw," she said, examining her own palms carefully now.

"She didn't give you a reading?"

"I didn't ask, and she didn't offer."

Stephen sat down again and showed her his left palm. "My love line," he said, "is cut short here." He pointed to a short line less than an inch long that cut diagonally across his palm. "Annabel told me it meant we weren't going to be together for long. But look at yours!" He placed his left hand next to her right, so the lines made a bridge across their palms. "You have a short one, too. But where mine stops, yours begins!"

His voice dropped to a whisper as he gazed at her. "Love lost … and found again."

Taylor didn't know what to say. She felt an anxious fluttering in her stomach. Strangely, she found she couldn't take her eyes off of Stephen. Was it a piece of Annabel's spirit trying to connect again to her old love, or something else?

She glanced at the photograph. Annabel, just as young and pretty as she'd been in her car but without the burden of the grave, grinned at her from the front seat of a red Camaro.

He's the one, you know, she'd told Taylor with the full confidence and hopefulness of youth. *I feel it deep inside. I couldn't live without him.*

"I'm sorry," Stephen said quickly, backing away. "I'm acting foolish. You must want to get going." But his gaze kept burning straight into hers. After several seconds passed with neither of them saying anything, Taylor said, "Thank you for the coffee. I really should be going." She stood and headed for the door.

"Of course." Stephen stood, reaching for the door. "If you're ever going by this way again, stop in and say hi. Coffee's always on."

She walked past him and smiled. "I visit my sister often. This isn't exactly a short cut, but …" She found herself glancing at the shortened love line on her hand. The one made complete by Stephen's. "But I'd like to see you again. I think Annabel was right."

"About what?"

I think he might be the one you've been waiting for.

"I'll tell you later," she said, and stepped down off the porch into a perfectly clear, moonlit night.